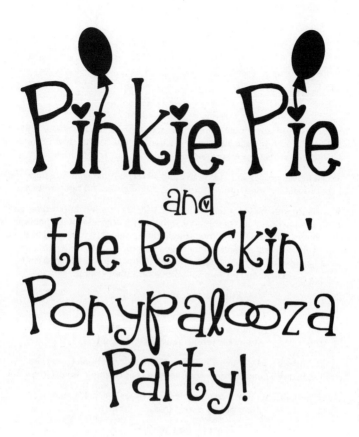

Pinkie Pie and the Rockin' Ponypalooza Party!

Written by G. M. Berrow

Little, Brown and Company

New York ✳ Boston

Little, Brown and Company

Hachette Book Group
1290 Avenue of the Americas, New York, NY 10104
Visit our website at www.lb-kids.com

Little, Brown and Company is a division of Hachette Book Group, Inc.
The Little, Brown name and logo are trademarks of Hachette Book Group, Inc.

The publisher is not responsible for websites (or their content)
that are not owned by the publisher.

First Edition: July 2013

Library of Congress Control Number: 2013931573

ISBN 978-0-316-22818-3

10 9 8 7 6 5 4 3 2

RRD-C

Printed in the United States of America

To Merm—my true rock

CONTENTS

* * *

CHAPTER 1

Welcome, Spring-Sproing Springtime

★ ★ ★

It was a perfect day in Ponyville. The clouds finally cleared from the sky and gentle rays of sunshine illuminated every cottage, garden, and cobblestone path. Ponies all around town emerged from their homes, blinking the sleepy winter out of their eyes. It had been almost a week since they'd finished their annual Winter Wrap-Up. The ponies had spent an entire day working hard to clear the paths of snow and ice, welcoming back the critters, and plowing the fields to ready them for crops of fresh fruits and veggies. Now every morning was like opening a present! The ponies loved being greeted by flowers and butterflies, rather than snowflakes and chilly breezes.

This morning, one pony in particular was feeling an extra spring in her step.

"Waaaaaaaaake up, citizens of Ponyville!" Pinkie Pie hollered, throwing open her bedroom window on the tippity-top floor of Sugarcube Corner. She was oblivious to the early hour. Even though nopony was awake enough yet to listen, she called out, "It's going to be an awesome day!"

The candy-striped curtains rustled as a sweet, fresh breeze floated inside. Pinkie closed her eyes, inhaled deeply, and smiled from ear to ear. "Don't you just love spring, Gummy?" Pinkie bounced around her pet alligator with glee, her curly fuchsia mane puffing up. "It's all sunshine and good smells and playing outside!"

Gummy blinked his large eyes in response, but his face remained expressionless. "Here! Smell this! It'll make you feel all flowery-powery!" Pinkie plucked a purple posy from her newly installed window box and bounded back over to Gummy. The tiny gator opened his mouth, clamped down on the posy, and swallowed.

"Ooooh, what a fun way to welcome spring, Gummy! Maybe I'll try it, too."

Pinkie plucked another bloom and popped it into her mouth. Her face twisted into a sour look. It did *not* taste like a sugary delight. "Yuck! Actually, maybe I'll just stick to cupcakes for now."

Pinkie trotted across the brightly colored room. Everything in sight was patterned with hearts or balloons. "So, what's on the PPP for today, Gummy?" She looked over her Pinkie Party Planner on the wall. It had been a gift from Twilight Sparkle and was where she kept track of all the exciting parties happening around Ponyville. The majority of them were events she'd planned herself, but it still pleased her to see how much fun everypony was having. Ever since she accidentally multiplied herself in the Mirror Pool in an attempt not to miss out on anything, she thought it was best to keep track of fun another way.

She scanned the list. "Let's see...Ice-Cream Sundae Sunday party at Sweetcream Scoops's house? No, that's tomorrow. Silly me! Today is Saturday." She looked at Saturday—but what Pinkie saw there horrified her. There weren't *any* parties on today's schedule. Not one! Pinkie's jaw dropped, and she sunk to the floor like a wilted flower. How could this be? A whole day with no fun activities to attend? What was she going to do with her time? The sweet sound of birds chirping outside taunted her. Even the birds sounded like they had a party planned for today!

Pinkie stood up straight with a determined look in her eye. "There's no way we can waste such a prettiful sunshiny day doing *nothing*, Gummy!" She leaped over to a mountainous stack of colored boxes in the corner—her party supplies—and started to riffle through them rapidly. Neon streamers flew through the air. Glitter confetti sprinkled down. Pointed party hats, noisemakers, and birthday candles rolled across the floor. It looked like Pinkie's party cannon had exploded! She was making a big mess, but she didn't care. Pinkie Pie needed inspiration.

"Aha! This could be superiffic...." Pinkie squealed, pulling out a shiny magenta cape edged in blue and yellow ribbons. She threw it over her shoulders and popped on a matching mask. "A superpony party, perhaps?"

Gummy blinked, unconvinced. Pinkie's shoulders sagged. He was right. The cape wasn't quite doing it. Pinkie tossed it onto the pile of rejected items and sighed. "I know! I know!" she said, brightening up again. "How about a Capture the Flag tournament? Those are fantilly-astically fun!"

Pinkie grunted as she struggled to push a massive gold box labeled PARTY FLAGS! (1 OF 3) to the center of the room. She placed a small ladder on the side and dived head-first into the box, causing several flags to spill out and land on the already cluttered floor.

Pinkie wasn't just looking for any old flag. She wanted a special flag that would be absolutely perfect for the game, and she knew just the one. It was a keepsake from the time she'd been in charge of the flügelhorn booth at the Crystal Faire. It had a sparkly pink flügelhorn on it. Sparkles were very popular in Equestria lately—ever since the Crystal Empire had returned.

But it was no use! Pinkie found checkered racing flags, some Summer Sun Celebration flags, and even flags with tiny flags painted on them. But no pink flügelhorn. Pinkie was pretty down on her luck today. "Oh well. Never mind that!" she exclaimed. "I'm sure there's something else around here...."

Meanwhile, Gummy climbed on top of one of Pinkie's homemade Super Spring Sneakers—a set of shoes with giant silver springs attached to the bottoms for maximum bounce-ability. He slowly sprang up and down on one of them, and the shoe made a small squeaky noise. It was hard to tell if he was having fun, since he couldn't smile, but he kept doing it, so that was a good indication.

"Gummy, you're brilliant!" Pinkie shouted. She did a celebratory twirl that rustled up some stray confetti like a party tornado. "Why didn't you say something sooner?!" Pinkie smiled extra wide and strapped on her sneakers. "We're going to have a Spring-Sproing-Spring Party to welcome the new season! We have so much to do!" And with that, Pinkie bounced out the door and into action. It was time to get this party started!

CHAPTER 2

Pinkie's Party Ponies

★ ★ ★

Whenever Pinkie Pie went somewhere, it usually took her much less time than other ponies. She had a unique way of traveling. She preferred to hop, skip, or bounce rather than trot or walk. Today, with her spring-loaded sneaks strapped to her hooves, she was bouncing high into the sky. "Hellooo!"

she chirped as she poked her head through a cloud, surprising a green Pegasus with a yellow mane who had been asleep.

Boing! B-b-ba-doing! Boing! B-b-ba-doing!

Within a few minutes, Pinkie accidentally found herself on the outskirts of Ponyville. "Whoopsy-doodles! I overshot my bounce range again!" She giggled before heading back to the spot where she had meant to land—right in the center of Ponyville. It was the absolute best spot to start telling every-pony about the Spring-Sproing-Spring Party. Then she would quickly go cottage to cottage, leaving plenty of time to set up for the party and have the best time ever the rest of the day.

Pinkie cleared her throat and looked out into the now-bustling marketplace. She began to sing and do a bubbly dance rou-tine. "It's spring! It's spring! What a wonderful thing! It's time to laugh; it's time to sing! But most of all…it's time to spriiiiiiiiing!" Pinkie Pie spread her hooves out wide and smiled at the crowd.

But nopony had stopped to listen. That didn't stop Pinkie. "You're all invited to my Spring-Sproing-Spring Party! This afternoon! By the lake! Be there if you like having a little fun, a lot of fun, or even just medium fun!"

Sea Swirl and Rose trotted past, giggling and shaking their heads. They were used to seeing Pinkie act silly, and seemed to be too busy to stop and hear what the party was all about. Pinkie shrugged and started her song again. "It's spring! It's spring! What a won—"

All of a sudden, a little voice interrupted her.

"A party? Can we come, Pinkie?" said Apple Bloom in her cowgirl accent, jumping up and down like a baby lamb. She was just a little filly—light yellow-green with a bold pink mane. She hadn't received her cutie mark yet. As usual, her two best friends, Scootaloo and Sweetie Belle—also "blank flanks," were standing by her side.

"Of course!" Pinkie shouted, and sprang into the air. "Everypony's invited! Especially you three!"

"Yay!" the three ponies chorused, and erupted into a tizzy of excitement. Parties in Ponyville were a frequent occurrence, but they weren't usually called out as guests of honor.

"What sort of awesome stuff will there be at the party?" asked Scootaloo. "Will there be bouncing?"

"Will there be springing?" added Sweetie Belle.

"What about sproinging?" squealed Apple Bloom.

"All of the above!" shouted Pinkie, her smile growing wider by the second. "And also big huge trampolines, a bouncy barn, and bundles of bungees! All of the springiest things there are." Pinkie looked at them proudly.

"Well, count the Cutie Mark Crusaders in," said Apple Bloom. She turned to her two friends. "Maybe one of us will get our cutie mark while we're there!"

"Yeah!" Scootaloo chimed in. "My hidden talent could be . . . jumping?"

"Let's find out!" Pinkie pulled three sets of mini spring-loaded shoes just like hers seemingly out of nowhere. It was almost like magic, but it wasn't—it was just Pinkie. She was prepared for a good time, and nopony could blame her for that!

"Wow, these are for us?" Apple Bloom took a pair and put them on her hooves. She hesitantly gave a little bounce and nearly lost her footing. It wasn't as easy as Pinkie made it look!

Pinkie's face became serious. "I need you to help me out. Everypony in town looks so busy, but I don't want them to miss this beautiful new spring day! Can you go around Ponyville and spread the word about the party while I get everything ready?"

"We'll do it!" the Cutie Mark Crusaders said in unison. They loved a new challenge, especially if a party awaited them at the other end.

"Awesome!" Pinkie replied with a jump.

"I've always wanted some Party-Planning Ponies!"

The three fillies puffed up with pride.

"Okay." Pinkie pointed to Sweetie Belle. "You start by finding your sister. Go!" Sweetie Belle nodded and bounced toward Rarity's home and shop, the Carousel Boutique. Rarity was probably there right now, working on some new outfits.

"Scootaloo, you head toward Rainbow Dash's cloud and tell her about the party so she can tell everypony in Cloudsdale!" Scootaloo nodded and started off. She couldn't fly yet, but the bouncy shoes gave her a little more height with each step. Scootaloo flitted her tiny wings hopefully and disappeared into the distance.

"And you, Apple Bloom," Pinkie said, looking down at her little filly friend, "are in charge of rounding up the entire Apple family! Yippee!"

"Aw, man," said Apple Bloom, scuffing the dirt with her hoof. "Can't I go somewhere different than my house? Somewhere excitin'?"

Pinkie cocked her head to one side, pondering this. Of course Apple Bloom didn't want to go to Sweet Apple Acres—she spent every day and night there! "You make an excellent point, Apple Bloom," Pinkie agreed. "Going to *new* places is way more fun! Why don't you take the path to Fluttershy's and stop at Twilight's library on the way?"

"I'm on it!" Apple Bloom was off before Pinkie could say "Meet me by the lake!"

Pinkie smiled in satisfaction. She was glad that her little Party Ponies understood how important the party was going to be.

CHAPTER 3

The Road Less Sparkled

★ ★ ★

Before heading to Sweet Apple Acres to invite Applejack, Pinkie decided to take a mini detour. She would first stop by Cheerilee's house, Sweetie Drops's cottage, and Cranky Doodle Donkey's place. (Just in case he wanted to play, for *once*. He usually didn't, but Pinkie always asked anyway. It was the right thing to do.)

As Pinkie Pie bounced up the cobble-stoned path to Cheerilee's house, humming an upbeat tune, she noticed something shiny on the ground. Pinkie bent down from her tall shoes to examine the mysterious glimmer. "I spy with my little Pinkie Eye, something SHINY!" Upon closer inspection, she saw that it was none other than a rich red ruby! Sunshine reflected off its facets and made it appear extra gorgeous next to the dull gray rocks of the path.

"Wowza!" exclaimed Pinkie. "Sparkly-warkly prettiness!" Getting excited over a ruby made her feel like Rarity, who had a special talent for finding precious stones with her magic. Pinkie had many talents, but that wasn't one of them. Yet there was the little stone—just sitting on the path. But what was a ruby doing there? How peculiar....

Maybe somepony had dropped it! Pinkie looked around. There wasn't a soul in sight. "Come with me, little ruby!" Pinkie said to the stone. "I'll help you find your owner again. I bet somepony is missing you real bad!"

Pinkie tried to pick it up, but the ruby wouldn't budge. Pinkie pulled and twisted every which way, but it remained stuck to the ground. Suddenly, she let go of the gem and toppled hooves over head into the nearby hedge. Her springy shoes had bounced her backward!

Pinkie popped out of the bush and looked again. The ruby really was stuck to the path.... But why? Just then, Pinkie noticed lots of other sparkles all around her. The path seemed to be dotted with colorful gemstones wedged between the normal gray, black, and white rocks. They looked like rainbow sprinkles on a giant cupcake. It was such a pretty sight!

"Ooooh…ahhhh…" cooed Pinkie, her smile widening in genuine delight. "What a fun new way to spruce up a front garden." Pinkie started to hop from stone to stone, looking down at the spectrum of precious gems in awe. "Hey there, Emerald! How's it going, Sapphire?"

Just then, a mauve-colored pony with a light pink mane and a cutie mark of three smiling daisies opened the door. "Pinkie Pie!" she called out. "I thought I heard somepony outside."

"Hiya there, Cheerilee! I was just talking

to your gems!" Pinkie bounced over. "Your front path is like a party under your hooves!"

"Thanks, Pinkie! I just installed it. New garden gems from the Crystal Empire. I didn't want to be one of those ponies who follow all the Canterlot trends, but this one is just so lovely." Cheerilee smiled shyly. She was usually a no-frills sort of pony, but apparently even she couldn't resist some glitz and glamour once in a while. Pinkie wondered if Rarity had caught onto the trend yet.

"Abso-tootley-lutely!" Pinkie agreed, bouncing up and down. Cheerilee gave Pinkie's springy shoes a strange look. It wasn't out of the ordinary to see Pinkie wearing something different, but this was especially odd.

"So, what brings you to my house this morning?"

Pinkie smiled. "Well, since you asked...
do you like having a little fun, a lot of fun,
or even medium fun?!"

Cheerilee considered the question. "Well,
I guess if you are twisting my hoof, I'd have
to choose 'a lot of fun.'"

"Guhhh-reat!" Pinkie answered. "Because
you're invited to my first-ever, totally awesome Spring-Sproing-Spring Party! It's to
welcome spring, and it's guaranteed to be
any level of fun you want!"

Cheerilee laughed. "I'll be there." Pinkie's
constant enthusiasm was pretty contagious,
even if a bit tiring. "What would Ponyville do
without all your parties, Pinkie?"

Pinkie shuddered at the thought. Imagining a Ponyville with no parties was horrible.
"It would probably be really, really, really
boring!" she said, snapping out of her day-

dream. "See ya later, Cheerilee! Bring friends! Bring bunnies! Bring bouncy things!"

As the excited pony took off, it was hard to tell which thing shone more—the pretty path or Pinkie Pie herself.

CHAPTER 4

The Spring-
Sproing-Spring
Party!

★ ★ ★

"What in Equestria will Pinkie dream up next time?" Twilight Sparkle said to Fluttershy. "Look at this place!" The two pony friends stood on the sidelines of the

Spring-Sproing-Spring Party, taking in the splendor and warm spring sunshine.

As Pinkie had promised, the whole area by the lake was decorated in a springy theme. Corkscrew streamers and ribbons hung from the trees. Three massive pink trampolines were set up, along with a bouncy barn, jump ropes, a big bin of bungees, and a bunny bed. It was, indeed, the springiest place anypony had ever seen.

"I can't believe Pinkie Pie put all this together in just one day! She's so talented," Fluttershy said in her soft voice. "And Angel Bunny sure is having fun with his friends." She pointed to the area where about twenty-five bunnies were hopping up and down on a mattress, giggling. Nearby, Rainbow Dash was taking her turn on one of the trampolines.

"And look at Rainbow over there," added Applejack, trotting up and joining them. "She sure knows how to put on an excitin' show!" Rainbow did a triple backflip, and all the ponies waiting in line cheered.

"Totally cool, Rainbow!" squeaked Scootaloo. Rainbow Dash was her idol, and Scootaloo thought anything she did was awesome.

"Do it again!" shouted Lemon Hearts, a yellow unicorn with a sky-blue mane. Rainbow didn't miss a beat. She called out, "You think that was cool? I can do another trick that's at least forty percent cooler!"

A moment later, she launched herself into another triple flip routine that would have shamed any circus pony. She jumped high into the sky, burst through a fluffy cloud, and somersaulted back down to the trampoline—all without the use of her wings. The crowd cheered once more.

"Wheeee!" Pinkie Pie bounced up to her friends, still wearing her shoes with the giant springs on them. "Hey, girls! Isn't this party hoppin'?" Pinkie began to laugh. "Get it? *Hoppin'!*"

"You could say that, all right," replied Applejack. "I think I'm gonna go for a jump on that bouncy barn. Looks almost like the one we have at home! Except it's inflatable."

"Of course it does! I designed it based on the one at Sweet Apple Acres. You wanna know why? Huh? Huh? Huh?!" Pinkie asked, nodding her head. "Because he's the friendliest barn I know. You sure raised him well, Applejack!"

"I wasn't aware you knew a lot of barns

personally, Pinkie," Twilight joked. It amused her that Pinkie was now making friends with buildings, along with everypony in town. What was next? Hanging out with vegetables? A picnic with trees?

"Oh, I *do*," said Pinkie. She began talking really fast. "You'd be surprised! Let's see…there's the rock farm barn, the barn at Nana Pinkie's, the barn at Granny Pie's—that one's a *little* grumpy—and a gazillion trillion more!" Her mane was puffed up to full height, which meant that Pinkie was very excited. Either that, or she'd just been jumping a lot. Or both. "So, have you guys tried any of the super-fun activities yet?!"

Rarity, who had joined them in the middle of Pinkie's barn speech, sighed loudly. "Oh, you know I normally would, darling, except I just can't stand the thought of having to fix my mane afterward. Jumping and perfect hair do *not* go together!" She flicked her shiny purple coif to illustrate her point and trotted off to go check out her reflection in the lake.

"Okeydokey-lokey!" Pinkie replied, unfazed. "Catch ya later, Rarity!"

Twilight shrugged, then watched as Spike dived off the bungee platform, laughing as he sprang back up like a baby dragon–sized yo-yo. "Well, Pinkie, I'd say your Spring-Sproing-Spring Party is a smashing success," she said. "It seems like everypony in town is here! Even someponies I've never seen before. Like that group over there." Twilight gestured toward the bouncy barn where an older couple stood with their two daughters.

The old stallion had a light brown coat and gray mane with long sideburns and wore an old-fashioned pilgrim hat and tie. His wife had a light gray coat and wore her dark gray mane tied up in a tight bun, along with glasses and a stern expression on her face. The two young mares with them were different shades of gray. Their manes were both bone-straight, but one of them had her bangs cut evenly across and the other had hers flipped over the side of her face. They looked at each other and then frowned at the festivities going on around them.

Twilight furrowed her brow, wondering why the family was acting so odd. "Maybe they are new to Ponyville, or they are just passing through?" Something about their look said that these weren't really urban ponies. They seemed so confused and lost.

The two young ponies looked up at the large inflatable barn like they'd never even seen one before.

"New ponies? Oh boy, oh boy! Where? Where?!" shouted Pinkie Pie, darting across the field. She loved nothing more than welcoming new residents to town and learning every single thing about them. A pony could never have too many friends! Pinkie ran back and forth, scanning the crowd until her eyes landed on the group in question. The smile on her face instantly grew to maximum Pinkie happiness.

"I don't believe this!" Pinkie screamed with joy. She bounced up to the top of the bungee platform and pulled out a glittery pink megaphone. "Fillies and gentlecolts! Your attention, puuuuh-lease!"

Everypony stopped jumping and turned

to Pinkie for her big announcement. "I'd like you all to welcome to Ponyville...my FAMILY! Look, look! It's really them!" Pinkie threw confetti onto the crowd of townsponies and a cheer rang out. "See?! That's my mom, Cloudy Quartz, and my dad, Igneous Rock! And my two sisters—Marble Pie and Limestone Pie!" The crowd craned their necks to get a look at the newcomers.

"That's Pinkie Pie's family?" Spike said to Twilight. "But they don't look anything like her!"

"Maybe they are one of those families that are similar in other ways," Twilight suggested. They did look a bit plain to have such a kooky daughter like Pinkie. But families came in all shapes, sizes, and colors.

"Yaaaaaaay! Familyyyyyy!" Pinkie jumped onto one of the trampolines, using it as a launch pad to land right in front of her sisters. Pinkie couldn't believe how her luck had turned around today. She loved parties and she loved surprises....But a visit from her parents and sisters at one of her parties? That was the biggest surprise of all!

CHAPTER 5

Between a Rock Farm and a Hard Place

★ ★ ★

Her family all wore blank expressions as Pinkie skipped and twirled with glee. It was obvious that Igneous Rock had dealt with Pinkie's exhausting energy many times before when she was a filly. He stood patiently for a while, waiting for her to calm down. But soon he grew tired of the act, and his face morphed into a frown. "All right, now," he said. "That's enough." But Pinkie was too excited to notice his disapproval.

Meanwhile, Twilight, Applejack, Flutter-shy, Rainbow Dash, and Rarity stood close by. They'd heard a lot about Pinkie's days growing up on the rock farm, but they'd never actually met Pinkie's family before. Some of the other party-going ponies started to gather around, too. Apparently, they were also curious to learn more about the rela-tions of the most popular pony in town. Chances were good that her family was probably totally fun, too.

"Hi, Mom! Hey there, Dad! How's it going, Marble? What's new, Limestone? Where's—?"

"Your older sister is keeping an eye on the farm," Igneous cut her off.

"Oh, okay. So what are you guys doing here?! I'm so totally surprised!" Pinkie skipped around her family. "My Pinkie Sense didn't warn me about this at all! Are you here to party? I planned all this! Look, there are lots of really cool—"

"Pinkamena Diane Pie," Igneous interrupted. "We are not here to party."

Pinkie stopped in her tracks. "Oh. You're not?" She cocked her head to one side.

"No," Cloudy Quartz replied. Marble and Limestone shook their heads solemnly.

"Well, why'd you show up at a party, then, you bunch of silly heads?" Pinkie giggled and nudged her mother. "A party is the absolute *worst* place to *not* party!"

A couple of ponies laughed. Pinkie did have a pretty good point there.

"Pinkamena, don't you start with me...." Cloudy warned, looking down at Pinkie through her glasses. Pinkie shrank back.

"Sorry, ma'am," Pinkie said, her mane deflating a little. "I just got really excited to see you guys. It's been super-duper long! I mean, you guys never even leave the rock farm. Oh no—is something wrong with Rockie?!"

"Who's Rockie?" Cloudy asked, growing impatient.

"Rockie's my pet rock, Mom! He's gray and a bit lumpy and about yay big?" Pinkie made a motion with her hooves to demonstrate the size of the rock in question. "I definitely introduced you to him."

"Oh," replied Cloudy Quartz.

"Anyway, I only left him back at the farm

because he said he'd miss all of his rock buddies," Pinkie explained to her friends. She turned back to her parents. "Marble and Limey promised to look after him!"

Marble Pie's face remained blank. Limestone Pie blinked. *Plink, plink.*

Igneous cleared his throat and started to pace back and forth across the grass. "This here has got nothin' to do with pet rocks or parties, Pinkamena."

"Well...why are you guys in Ponyville, then, Dad? Huh? Huh? Huh?" Pinkie looked to the faces of her family but couldn't read them at all. "Oooh, let me guess! Are we going on a family vacation to Appleloosa? Or...I know, I know! You came to bring me some of Granny Pie's scrumptious rock cakes!" Pinkie looked around, but her family hadn't brought any satchels with them.

"No, that's not it.... Okay, okay, I give up! Tell meeeee!" Pinkie's eyes were practically popping out of her head with excitement.

"Your mother, sisters, and I are here for a very important reason," Igneous began. Pinkie frowned. Whatever it was, it didn't sound very fun at all. In fact, it sounded . . . *serious.*

"Well, word got 'round that you are friends with—" Igneous looked around nervously, realizing he had an audience of curious Ponyville residents watching his every move. "We heard that you might know . . ." Igneous puffed up his chest and finally announced, "We are here to see Her Royal Highness, Princess Twilight Sparkle, regarding a very urgent business matter!"

"We need to see the princess," Cloudy said. The sisters nodded in unison.

Pinkie's face dropped. "You're not here

to party *or* to see me?" She pouted, slumping down to the ground like a deflated balloon. "This is the worst surprise ever!"

"I'm sorry, but we have to talk to the princess and then get back to the farm right away," Cloudy replied. "We don't have time for any of this party nonsense right now."

"Oh, I see." Pinkie sighed.

"It's not nonsense!" Twilight said, stepping forward. "And I'm right here."

Everypony turned to look at Twilight, who up until now had been happily blending into the crowd. Usually, when she was at home in Ponyville, she preferred that everypony treat her like they did before she became a princess. None of this "Your Royal Highness" mumbo jumbo that every other pony in Equestria insisted on. Twilight still wasn't used to all the attention, but she would do anything to help a friend, and it seemed like Pinkie needed her to play the princess role today.

Twilight straightened and spoke in her most regal voice. "Welcome to our fair Ponyville." She bowed as she had seen Celestia and Cadance do.

Igneous, Cloudy, Marble, and Limestone immediately bowed their heads and leaned their front hooves on the grass to show their respect. "Princess!" Igneous Rock said, standing up again. "Thank you for having us. We'd be so grateful if you'd help us out."

"I'll help in any way that I can, Mr. Rock," Twilight said. Then she added, "Pinkie is, after all, one of my *very best friends*." Cloudy and the sisters looked down at their hooves, a little embarrassed for the way they'd just treated Pinkie in front of royalty.

"That's great news, Your Royal Highness," said Igneous, taking off his hat. But he didn't sound too chipper. In fact, despair was written all over his face. "It's great news...because we are about to lose the rock farm." The crowd gasped, even though most of them hadn't known the farm existed until then. It just seemed like the right response.

"What?!" Pinkie Pie shouted, practically leaping into the air.

"How dreadful!" exclaimed Rarity.

"Major bummer!" remarked Rainbow Dash.

"Oh, that's really too bad," whispered Fluttershy. "Those poor little rocks."

"Say, Pinkie, are you okay?" asked Applejack, giving her friend a sideways glance. "She looks a little...different, right?" she whispered to Rainbow Dash.

Pinkie did look strange all of a sudden. Her eyes were wide with terror, and she stood completely frozen to the spot. Fluttershy and Rarity exchanged concerned looks. Igneous Rock's news had been shocking to say the least, but they'd never seen Pinkie look so utterly...speechless.

"Somepony poke her or something!" said Rarity. "I've never seen her stand still before. It's so strange!"

Spike ran over and gave her a gentle nudge. "Uhhh, you okay, Pinkie?"

Pinkie looked up, her face full of sadness. "Everypony go home," she said, casting her eyes down at the ground. "This party is...over." Everypony gasped. Nopony ever expected to hear Pinkie Pie say such a thing.

CHAPTER 6

The Pink Sheep of the Family

★ ★ ★

Pinkie Pie had always been the silliest, most fun-loving pony in town. If she was that upset over the closing of a rock farm, then it must be a big deal. For the rest of the day, every-pony was abuzz with gossip and chatter about how Pinkie Pie herself had actually broken up a party! What was Equestria coming to?

"But I thought she didn't even *like* the rock farm!" Rarity whispered to Rainbow Dash. They were following Applejack as she led Pinkie's family over to the big barn at Sweet Apple Acres.

"Well, the rock farm was her home, so she's probably sad it will be gone," Flutter-shy offered in her tiny, gentle voice. Her pink mane fell over one of her pretty blue eyes. "I can't imagine such a thing."

"I guess there's no place like *stones*?" Rainbow joked. "Okay, okay, I'll admit it— that was bad."

"Hey, are those emeralds around the flower border?" Rarity gasped, trotting up to the barn entrance. She was easily dis-tracted by gemstones, no matter where they were. "How *divine*!"

"Come on inside, y'all," Applejack said,

ushering her friends and Pinkie's family inside.

"At least we'll have a li'l bit of privacy in here." She peeked her head out the barn door to make sure there were no stray party ponies following them. The Pie sisters looked at their surroundings in awe. Everything seemed to be so much brighter in Ponyville than back home.

"Good call, A.J. Now, where were we?" Twilight walked over and hugged Pinkie. Luckily, she had started to perk up after Apple Bloom brought her an Emergency Cupcake. Thank goodness Pinkie had recently installed a few pink glass cases around Ponyville for situations just like this one. A cupcake was an instant cheerer-upper.

"What happened to the farm, Mr. Rock? And what can *all of us* here in Ponyville do to help?" Twilight wanted to make sure the family understood just how important her friends were to her. Being a princess required lots of support. It wasn't just a one-pony job.

Igneous sat down on a wooden bench and hung his head. It looked like he had the weight of the whole rock farm on his shoulders. Marble, Limestone, and Cloudy Quartz trotted over and sat beside him. They all looked really sad.

"Go on now, Iggy," Cloudy said with her slight country twang. She patted her husband on the back. "Tell the princess here what's goin' on."

"Why don't you explain, Cloudy?" he said, looking tired.

"Yeah! Tell us, Mom!" Pinkie said, jumping up and down. She couldn't take the suspense any longer. "Tell us now!"

"Calm down, for granite's sake," Cloudy replied. "I'll tell ya!"

But before she could begin, Limestone blinked her eyes and cleared her throat. "It's the gems!" she blurted out.

"The gems?" Rarity asked. Any mention of jewels always piqued her interest. "What about them?"

"Ever since that Crystal Empire showed up again, all anypony wants are stones that shine, sparkle, and shimmer!" Cloudy explained. She cast her eyes down to the floor in defeat, and her bottom lip started to quiver. "Plain old rocks are boring."

"No, they're not, Mom!" Pinkie cut in. "Rocks are so totally awesome! There's slate!

And granite! And marble! And mudstone! And—"

"Well, you tell that to the rest of Equestria," Marble Pie replied. "We haven't had any business for months!"

"That's awful!" said Twilight. She felt especially bad, thinking of all she had done for the Crystal Empire. She never expected the rest of Equestria to be affected by its return, especially by turning ponies out of their homes.

Pinkie suddenly recalled that very morning when she'd seen Cheerilee's gem-lined front path. And Rarity had just pointed out that the Apple family had put in some gems around the barn. Now that Pinkie thought about it, it did seem like a lot of ponies right there in Ponyville were really into jewels lately. But Pinkie Pie never considered how that trend could be a problem for anypony, let alone her own family.

Pinkie looked at the sad faces of her two sisters and her parents. The gravity of the situation hit her like a ton of rocks. She had to do something, *anything*, to help them! Pinkie may have left her rock-farming days behind her, but the last thing she wanted was for her family to lose the farm. She pictured the old barn, the rock fields, and the drab gray landscape. It wasn't much, but it was home. *Thinkie, Pinkie!* she said to herself. She thought extra hard.

And then it came to her.

Pinkie began trotting around the barn, skipping and shouting. "I know! I know!" She did a grand leap and landed right in front of her parents. A puff of dirt and hay from the ground billowed up around her, and Limestone sneezed. "We'll throw a party!"

Pinkie Pie announced. "Then nopony will take you guys for granite anymore! Get it?! For *granite*!" She laughed.

Applejack and Rainbow Dash chuckled.

"A party?" asked Cloudy Quartz. She furrowed her brow in disapproval. "I don't know about that...."

"Yeah! But not just *any* party, Mom!" Pinkie said, growing more excited by the second. "A party dedicated to the total amazingness of rocks! It will be...a rock...a rock concert! We'll get bands and all sorts of rocks to decorate and invite everypony from every city all over Equestria to our very own PONY-PALOOZA!" Pinkie smiled wide and spread her arms as if to say "ta-da!"

Twilight, Rainbow Dash, Applejack, Fluttershy, and Rarity all turned to Pinkie's family for some sort of reaction. Marble frowned.

Limestone blinked. Cloudy winced. And Igneous remained stone-faced.

"What a splendid suggestion, Pinkie!" Rarity finally said, breaking the silence. "What do you think, Mr. Rock?"

"I think…" Igneous said, stepping forward. "That it's…"

Everypony leaned forward in anticipation of what he would say. "It's…"

Pinkie's smile grew with excitement.

"It's…the silliest idea I've ever heard in m' life! This is not something one of your parties can fix. Why can't you be serious for once, Pinkamena?"

"Well, I just thought that it could be super fun if—"

"Fun?" Igneous interrupted. "Why don't you go run along now and leave us alone with the princess so we can figure this out for real?"

Marble flipped her straight gray bangs, and nodded in agreement with her father.

Pinkie's face fell. All she'd wanted to do was help—and in the best way she knew how. And ever since she'd left the rock farm to live in Ponyville, parties had been her whole entire life. Pinkie Pie loved nothing more than to make other ponies smile. Usually, a little laughter and fun could ease even the worst problems!

It had even worked the day Pinkie had gotten her cutie mark. She'd thrown her very first party for the whole Pie family, and they'd all laughed and danced and smiled! So why wasn't it working now?

Pinkie looked to each of their faces. Nopony was smiling. Maybe they were right. Maybe she did need to stop being so silly all the time. Maybe it was time to be a little more serious.... If it meant that much to her family, then it meant that much to her. She made a decision right then and there.

"Mom, Dad," Pinkie Pie said, looking to her parents. "I, Pinkamena Diane Pie, *Pinkie Promise* to be a super-serious daughter from now on and not to throw any more parties! Cross my heart, hope to fly, stick a cupcake in my eye!"

Pinkie's friends looked at one another in shock. There was nothing in Equestria that would make Pinkie Pie break a Pinkie Promise! The situation with the rock farm had just gone from gravelly to grave.

CHAPTER 7

Pinkamena Serious Pie

★ ★ ★

As soon as Pinkie Pie woke up the next morning, she went straight to work on becoming the new Pinkie she had promised to be.

"No more messing around, Gummy!" she said to her pet alligator. "I'm Pinkamena *Serious* Pie now. Please don't bother me with any party invitations or fresh cupcake offers.

No swimming in the lake or dressing in silly costumes. All my time will henceforth be devoted to finding a super-duper serious way to save the rock farm!"

Pinkie trotted over to the mirror on the wall next to her Pinkie Party Planner and took a look at her reflection. Her hair had already fallen a little flat against her head, almost as straight as Marble's and Limestone's. But she still needed something else to look really serious.

Luckily, the mess she'd made the day before while trying to find a party inspiration still covered the floor. There were flags and party horns and costumes all over the place. Pinkie immediately spotted a great accessory for her new persona.

"These are perfect!" Pinkie said to herself, snapping the goofy fake nose and mustache off her favorite pair of joke glasses and popping the frames onto her face. "Now I look like I mean business."

Pinkie ripped down the Pinkie Party Planner and replaced it with a plain white calendar. It had lots of blank space to fill with important meetings and brainstorming sessions. "First on the Save the Farm schedule is to clean up this room! I can't have party hats and noisemakers distracting me if I am going to be thinking of really *serious* ways to save the farm." If she was going to focus, she couldn't be surrounded by such fun, colorful stuff! It all had to go. Pinkie got to work packing up all her party things in boxes. She didn't even bother to put each decoration and costume in the right place.

After Pinkie dragged the heavy boxes

down the Sugarcube Corner stairs, she got to work on the rest of the place. Pinkie had just started painting her room a drab shade of brown when she heard a hoof knocking on the door.

"Oooooh, a visitor!" Pinkie yelled out, forgetting to tone down her giddiness. "I'll be there in two shakes of a little lambie's tail!"

Pinkie dropped the paint roller into the pan, and it landed with a splat. Specks of brown paint splashed onto Gummy, who responded with his usual blink. Pinkie bounded to the door and flung it open.

Standing there was none other than Twilight Sparkle. She was wearing her princess crown, which was strange because she usually didn't unless she had to.

"Hellooooo, Twilight!" Pinkie sang out

with a singsongy lilt. She quickly realized that the greeting sounded far too excited and corrected herself. "I mean...ahem. Welcome, Ms. Sparkle. How may I help you this morning?" She tried to keep her voice monotone, like her sister Marble Pie. It wasn't *so*, so hard.

Twilight made a funny face. "So I guess you *were* serious about being serious, huh?" She stepped inside the room.

"Abso-tootley-lutely!" chirped Pinkie, then quickly added in her new voice. "I mean—yes, I am." She looked down at Twilight through her joke glasses.

"Why are you covered in chocolate, then?" Twilight asked, looking at the brown splotches all over Pinkie. Twilight didn't want to mention the odd glasses Pinkie was wearing. "Were you baking your famous double chocolate chip 'chipper' muffins again?" She hoped so. Twilight licked her lips just imagining the scrumptious taste of them. Pinkie was such a great baker.

"No, silly-willy Twilight!" Pinkie Pie said. "Look around! I'm redecorating! Or should I say... *undecorating*? Pinkamena Serious Pie would never have such a fun bedroom to play in. Once I fix all this stuff right up, finding a way to save the farm will be a piece of rock cake!"

"Undecorating?" Twilight said, suddenly noticing the blotchy brown paint all over the walls. What had Pinkie done? She loved her colorful bedroom! This situation was worse than Twilight thought. She had only ever seen Pinkie act this oddly one other time—when she and the gang had avoided going to Gummy's After-Birthday Party.

They'd only done it to plan a surprise party for Pinkie herself, but she'd gone all kooky. Pinkie had started talking to a sack of flour, some lint, a bowl of radishes, and a pile of rocks, claiming they were her best friends. This situation wasn't looking much better.

"Brown paint? No parties? Straight hair?" Twilight asked. "Pinkie, this isn't who you are! I came here to find you. We are going to plan the rock concert, just like you said! And we need your help."

"Thanks, but no thanks, Twilight!" Pinkie said, shaking her head. "You heard them....My family isn't interested in any more of my little parties. So I have to find another way to save the farm."

Pinkie picked up the paint roller again and began to paint. Her glasses didn't fit quite right and kept sliding down her nose.

Whenever she pushed them back up, she smudged more paint on her face. It looked super silly, but Twilight couldn't even laugh. Her friend was in trouble!

Twilight trotted to the door, feeling defeated. "Well, Pinkie, I guess it looks like *I'm* going to plan a Ponypalooza rock concert. Let me know if you have any suggestions!"

Maybe, just maybe, if Twilight showed Pinkie how much the ponies needed her help with the party, she wouldn't be able to resist.

CHAPTER 8

Pinkie-less Party Planning

★ ★ ★

It was unfortunate, but Twilight could already tell that Pinkie's family wasn't going to be much help, even though they'd finally agreed to let Twilight put on the show. Somehow, when they'd heard it from the princess's mouth, it seemed like a better idea than it had when Pinkie said it. But it was too late—they'd already hurt Pinkie's feelings, and now she was trying to be serious just to please them.

"All right, everypony. Let's put our brains together and try to figure out how exactly Pinkie Pie does this," Twilight Sparkle said to her friends. Twilight was surrounded by books on rocks, party planning, and rock music . . . but she had no idea where to start! Planning a rock concert was such a big task, and there wasn't much time. "Then we can figure out how to get Pinkie back to her normal silly self again."

Twilight picked up a purple book called *Geodes of Western Equestria* and began to read aloud. " 'A geode is a spherical stone that has a plain, rocklike appearance on the outside but on the inside contains a glittering, shiny center that consists of—' "

Rainbow Dash and Applejack exchanged a skeptical look.

"I'm sorry, Twi, but how is studying rock books going to help us plan a rock concert?" Rainbow Dash asked. Unless it was a Daring Do story, Rainbow didn't care too much for reading. "Shouldn't we be out there getting our hooves dirty?"

"Maybe we should try recruitin' some pony bands to perform at the show," offered Applejack. "I heard that Octavia might know the bassist from Nine Inch Tails."

"I could start on some decorations," said Fluttershy. "Or at least try to."

Twilight closed the book. "You ponies are right. This isn't getting us anywhere."

"Where are the Pie sisters? Surely, they have some opinions on the matter," Rarity said. "It is *their* party, after all!"

"I doubt it," answered Twilight as she began to use her magic to put away the stacks of books. Her horn sparkled, and the hardbacks floated gently up to their shelves, one by one. "If you haven't noticed, the Pies aren't too into parties. I only got the family to agree to let us put on the concert by telling them it was my official Royal Advice!"

"Where are they now?" asked Fluttershy, peeping out the window. "They looked so lost at the party yesterday."

Twilight nodded. "I completely agree. That's why Spike is giving them a tour of Ponyville. I told them that Spike was my Royal Tour Guide and it was a special honor to be shown around by him."

"They sure do look up to ya, huh?" Applejack said, pointing to Twilight's tiara. "Bein' a princess and all!"

"Now if only they'd believe me when I say the best pony for this job is Pinkie Pie!" exclaimed Twilight. "Then they'd see just how special she is to all of us here in Ponyville."

"Don't worry, Twi," said Rainbow Dash, looking smug. "Once we start putting the party together, Pinkie won't be able to help herself! I give her a few hours before she's in here calling all the shots."

Twilight looked down at her massive party to-do list. "Rainbow—you've just given me a great idea. I know exactly how to get Pinkie back!"

CHAPTER 9

Perusing Ponyville

★ ★ ★

"And this is where we all go to buy our quills and sofas," Spike told the visitors, standing in front of a little shop called Quills and Sofas. His presentation was met with little enthusiasm from Igneous Rock, who just stared back, chewing on a piece of hay.

"Is this where *the princess* buys her quills

and sofas?" Cloudy Quartz asked. Marble and Limestone listened intently.

"Yes, Twilight gets all her quills from here, too...." Spike groaned. Pinkie Pie's family certainly was starstruck by the idea of a royal pony in their midst. Every place they had visited, Cloudy had wanted to know Twilight's opinion on it. Marble and Limestone didn't say much; they just followed along. The two of them seemed to have an unspoken language that consisted mostly of blinks and nods.

"Does she send a lotta letters to Princess Celestia? To Canterlot?" Igneous questioned politely. "I've never been there m'self, but I hear it's real nice."

"Well, actually, I send the letters," Spike explained. "She tells me what to write, and I put it on the scrolls!"

"Is that so?" Igneous nodded his head and eyed Spike suspiciously as they continued. He still wasn't too used to hanging out with a talking baby dragon.

"I guess we can head to the Carousel Boutique next," Spike announced, leading the way. "Rarity owns it! She is known around Ponyville as the prettiest, um…I mean, most *fashionable* pony in town!" Spike still had a hard time containing his crush on Rarity. He blushed, but Pinkie's family didn't even notice. They had their sights on something else.

All of a sudden, Marble and Limestone gasped. Cloudy yelled out, "Iggy! Look at that over there!" They trotted over to Cheerilee's front walk and stared down at the glittering gems.

"This is what's puttin' us outta business!" Cloudy cried. "And I hate to admit it, but it does look *real* nice." The sisters crouched down to look at the jewels, much like Pinkie had done the day before. Cloudy started to cry. "We're doomed!"

Igneous hushed his wife. "Calm down, dear. We got a princess on our side now! She'll fix everythin' right up. Then we'll all be back to work on the rock farm before you know it."

Spike noticed Marble and Limestone Pie frown. They definitely looked like they could use a little less work and a little more play. Maybe they could come visit their sister more often and learn a thing or two about having fun. That is, if she ever switched back to normal....

"Oh, you're right, dear. Everythin's gonna be all right. Thank Celestia that Pinkamena is stayin' out of it like a good li'l filly," said

Cloudy, looking down at Igneous through her glasses. "You know how that girl gets an idea in her head and won't let it go."

"Mmmhmmm," Igneous Rock agreed, tipping his hat.

Spike felt bad for Pinkie. The way the whole family was treating her was ridiculous. She only wanted to help! And now she was driving herself bonkers trying to please them. Spike decided that the next stop on the tour had to be Sugarcube Corner. Maybe it would be just the thing to sweeten them up.

CHAPTER 10

A Visit to Sugarcube Corner

★ ★ ★

Pinkie had just finished changing all her bedroom accessories from bright, bold colors to shades of brown and gray when she heard somepony outside. She trotted over to the window. Down below, she spied with her little Pinkie Eye—her family! They were with Spike, who appeared to be gesturing wildly at Sugarcube Corner.

"Hey! Hey, parents! Up heeeeere!" Pinkie was excited to show them how serious she could be. "Look up here!" Pinkie shouted again.

Finally, they caught a glimpse of their transformed daughter. With her stick-straight mane and the glasses on her face, she was starting to look more like them again.

"Pinkamena! What are you doing up there?" Igneous shouted. The piece of hay he was chewing bobbed up and down in his mouth as he spoke. Cloudy Quartz squinted up at the window.

"This is where I live, family! Come up and see!" Pinkie shouted. She turned to Gummy and giggled. "Oh goody, goody rock hops! This is going to be fun! I mean—it's going to be . . . serious fun."

A moment later, Igneous, Cloudy, and Spike trotted inside the colorless room. Pinkie did a little twirl. "I *undecorated*! Just for you! Now I can be serious all the time!" Pinkie said, making a stern face. It didn't suit her.

"That's nice, dear. It's good to see you've made it look more like the barn back home. Is that Granny Pie's quilt over there?" Igneous pointed to the new blanket on Pinkie's bed—a gray-and-black creation with quilted rock shapes all over it.

"Oh yes," said Pinkie. "That's my basalt blankie, all right! Where are Marble and Limey? I want them to meet Gummy!"

"They are waiting downstairs, Pinkamena," her dad said, heading toward the door. "We don't have all day to just chat! We have business with the princess."

"Wait! You guys don't even want to hear my serious ideas to save the farm?" Pinkie said, looking crushed. "I have been thinking real hard all day!"

Cloudy patted Pinkie on the back before trotting out after her husband. "That's nice, dear. Tell us later on, ya hear?" Pinkie's shoulders slumped. Once again, Pinkie Pie had been unable to please her parents.

"Bye, Mom. Bye, Dad," Pinkie called out.

"Are you all right, Pinkie?" Spike asked, growing more concerned by the minute. "Are you sure you don't want to help Twilight and the girls with the party?"

There was a little glint in her eye, but it quickly passed. "I'm totally fine-eriffic, Spike. I'll just have to try harder! No parties! Pinkie never breaks a Pinkie Promise, remember, silly? Gotta go! See ya later, Spike!" Pinkie bounced out the door and down the stairs.

"Oh boy! That's what I was afraid of...." Spike said, looking at Gummy. "We gotta do something! Want to come with me to go find Twilight?" The little alligator blinked. "I'll take that as a yes!"

The Pinkie Trap

★ ★ ★

Rainbow Dash and Applejack stood in the middle of the road by Sugarcube Corner, waiting for Pinkie Pie to leave her house. "Are you sure this is going to work?" asked Applejack. She looked up at the big bunch of balloons she was holding in her hoof.

They looked pitiful. Every single one was misshapen or needed more helium.

"Are you kidding? Of course it will!" said Rainbow. "Look at these! There's no way Pinkie Pie will be able to stand how these balloons look. She'll want to show us how it's done. Then, she'll be reminded of how much she wants to help with the party and everything will be back to normal!" Rainbow pretended to brush some dust off her shoulder. "Easier than riding the Dizzitron at the Wonderbolt Academy."

"If you say so," Applejack said, craning her neck. They'd been standing there for quite a while. "I just hope we didn't miss her already."

"Miss who?" asked Pinkie Pie, who had somehow appeared right beside them. "Are you giving somepony a balloon surprise?"

Pinkie asked, struggling not to smile. She eyed the balloons hungrily.

"Well, not exactly..." Rainbow Dash said, playing along. "See...Applejack and I were just put in charge of balloons for the Pony-palooza party. How do these look, Pinkie? Perfect...*right*?" Rainbow paced around Pinkie like she was a royal guard interrogating a suspicious pony.

"Yeah, they're, um..." Pinkie started to sweat, and her eyes began to dart around. She looked at the balloons, desperate to say something. Her hair even started to puff up a little teensy bit. "They look just..."

"Yeah?" said Applejack. "How do they look?"

"They look guh-reat! Keep up the good work!" Pinkie said, regaining her focus. "No time to stay and chat! Serious business to take care of!"

Rainbow Dash and Applejack sunk down in defeat.

"Bye, Pinkie!" Rainbow called out, and then turned to Applejack. "I thought we had her for sure!"

"Don't worry. The others are ready to go," Applejack reminded her, watching Pinkie canter off into the distance.

As soon as Pinkie turned the corner by the Carousel Boutique, Rarity trotted outside to catch Pinkie. "Darling, I'm so glad I saw you passing by! I need your advice on these posters for the rock concert!" Rarity pulled out a large stack of hoof-made posters, covered in pictures of flowers and bows.

Pinkie scrunched up her nose. "They're nice and all, Rarity, but why the flowers and bows? It's a rock concert, silly!"

Rarity smiled. "Oh? Then what should I put on them?"

"Um...rock things?" Pinkie was using all her Pinkie Power not to explode into some sort of party monster right there. She was itching to take over, but she held fast to her promise to her family. "Actually, I think they are great just like that. Good luck with the posters, Rarity! See ya later!"

Rarity sighed as she watched her friend leave. "Well, I *tried*," she said to herself. "These posters are absolutely hideous!" She threw them up into the air, and they gently floated back down on top of her.

But Pinkie Pie was on a mission. She *needed* to get to the library. Little did Pinkie know, Twilight and some other guests were expecting her there, too.

A Peace of Pie

★ ★ ★

As Pinkie made her way to Twilight's home at the Golden Oak Library, she thought about how she'd resisted helping Rainbow and Applejack with those poorly inflated balloons. And then she'd stopped herself from redesigning Rarity's posters, even though they'd made no sense at all. While she couldn't believe her own Pinkie Power, she felt a little funny—and not in a good way. Why had she given up parties again? Pinkie was starting to forget the reason. She found herself imagining the right way to blow up a balloon and what sort of rock concert poster would look really awesome.

Focus, Pinkie! she thought as the library came into view. *You have to save the farm!* All she needed were a couple books, and Twilight just had to have them. Twilight was really smart, after all, and books were where she found most of her answers.

"Knock, knock, Twilight!" Pinkie shouted into the window. "I really, really, really, really need some books!"

"Come on in, Pinkie!" Twilight shouted from inside. "What sorts of things are you looking for?"

"Well, I'd like one on growing cucumbers and then one on how to run a rock circus and maybe a—" Pinkie pushed open the door, expecting to see just Twilight and Spike. Instead, she saw them—plus Rarity, Applejack, Rainbow Dash, Fluttershy, *and* Pinkie's whole family!

"Is this a surprise party?" Pinkie asked, her glasses sliding down her nose again. "Because I'm toooootally surprised!" Pinkie started to smile and then looked at her family and remembered why she had come there in the first place. "I mean, not that I like parties. I hate parties! *Blech*, parties are the worst thing ever!"

"You know that's not true, Pinkie Pie," said Twilight.

"Of course it is! I'm Pinkamena Serious Pie—the most serious-est pony in all of

Ponyville. Maybe even Equestria! Would anyone like to schedule a business meeting with me?" Pinkie pulled out a planner and pen and started scribbling furiously in it.

"No, but we would sure like our old friend Pinkie back," Applejack said, stepping forward. Rarity, Fluttershy, and Rainbow nodded in agreement.

"And we'd like our Pinkamena back, too," Igneous Rock said, joining them. He looked a little embarrassed, but he was smiling.

"You…you would?" Pinkie couldn't believe her ears. "But I thought…I thought that my parties were too silly for you! I thought you wanted me to be serious!"

"We're so sorry, Pinkamena, dear," Cloudy Quartz said. "We didn't mean to hurt your feelins'. We've just been under so much stress about losin' the farm and, well…we didn't think you'd understand. You've always had such a sunny outlook on things!"

"But I do understand! I do!" Pinkie said, taking off her glasses. "All I wanted to do was help!"

"We see that now, thanks to Princess Twi—thanks to all your *friends* here," said Igneous. "You're a real lucky pony. They were the ones who told us how you'd changed yerself just to please us. This talking baby dragon here was real concerned." Spike puffed out his chest.

"Well, Gummy and I were both worried," admitted Spike, patting the alligator on the head.

"We didn't realize what we had done until we saw you out the window just now, struggling to hold back your natural talent and not helping your friends."

Cloudy shook her head. "You don't need to do that ever again, sugar! We love you just as you are."

"Oh, family!" Pinkie felt herself bubbling over with happiness. She ran over to her family and scooped up all four of them in a big hug. "You guys are the bestie-westest!" When she pulled away from the embrace, her mane was at maximum poof. Pinkie Pie was back!

"Now that *that's* all over, we just have one question for you, Pinkie...." her mom said.

"What is it?!" Pinkie shouted, bouncing up and down. "Ask me! Ask me! Ask meeee!"

Igneous Rock cleared his throat. "Will you plan our rock concert party?"

Pinkie pretended to think about it. "Oh, all right. If you really want me to!"

Everypony cheered. Now they were really back in business.

CHAPTER 13

Pinkie Takes Action!

★ ★ ★

Pinkie snapped straight into action. It was all hooves on deck to rescue the party, and Pinkie could not have been happier. She bounced around the room, speaking a million words a minute. Her family stood by, amazed. Their eyes followed Pinkie as she darted back and forth, giving orders to everypony in the room. She was like a pin-ball in an arcade game.

"Rainbow Dash, you're in charge of the invitations! I'll need hundreds of tiny bags of rock candy with equally tiny parachutes on them! You can talk to Mrs. Cake about the candy and to Davenport at Quills and Sofas for the parachutes. Did you know he also does custom printing?! Little-known secret for those in the know. You and the other Pegasi take them all over Equestria! GO!" Rainbow nodded and rushed out the door.

Pinkie's mane was getting fluffier with each second. "Fluttershy, you call your old pal Photo Finish and tell her to bring in some of her famous friends! Spread the word that we need the biggest and rockingest bands in all of Equestria to perform! I want

every musician we know up on that stage—
Octavia! Lyra Heartstrings! DJ Pon-3! Lyrica
Lilac! Neigh-Z! Don't worry, though. I *also*
have some secret connections if those ponies
fall through!"

Pinkie winked at Twilight, who just looked
baffled. Nopony knew that Pinkie had celebrity friends. But she was full of surprises.

"Got it," Fluttershy said softly, and trotted out the door in a hurry.

"Applejack! Mom!" Pinkie shouted. "You're
next!"

"Me?" said Cloudy Quartz, looking around
as if there were some sort of mix-up.

"Totally!" Pinkie laughed. "You guys are
in charge of TREATS! I want apples. I want
rock cakes. I want apple rock cakes! Enough
to feed all of Equestria! Go, go, go!"

Applejack saluted Pinkie and led a very

confused Cloudy out of the cottage. "Come on, Mrs. Quartz! This is gonna be fun! We can go on a bakin' spree at Sweet Apple Acres!"

"Rarity! Twilight! Marble Pie! Limestone Pie!" Pinkie called out. The four ponies stepped forward, ready to receive their orders. "You ponies are in charge of... DECORATIONS!" Marble and Limestone exchanged an excited smile, finally allowing themselves a little fun. Their sister's enthusiasm was catching on!

"Oooh! That's just the job I wanted!" Rarity said, clapping her hooves together. "Okay, girls, I have so many ideas for the main stage curtains! I'm thinking velvet, maybe some gray satin? Black, shiny ropes and some marble columns? Going with sort of a rock-stone-chic look, you know?"

"That sounds amaaaaaazing!" Pinkie squealed. "The more rocks, the better!"

"Got it, Pinkie!" said Twilight, nodding. "Whatever you want!"

There was only one pony left without an assignment. Igneous Rock shuffled his hooves in the corner. "What should I do, Pinkamena?"

"Dad!" Pinkie bounced over to him. "You have the most important job of all!"

"I do?" he said, looking at his jubilant daughter. "What is it?"

Pinkie jumped into the air. "Have fuuu-uuun, of course!" she yelled before trotting out the door. "This totally rocks!"

CHAPTER 14

Pinkie Pie in the Sky

★ ★ ★

The roads to Ponyville were soon jammed with crowds of ponies from all over Equestria trying to make their way to the concert. The skies were busy with Pegasus traffic, and the Friendship Express train was at full capacity. It seemed like all of ponydom had come out for the party!

Pinkie watched in awe from high up in the sky. She was in Twilight's balloon, shouting greetings to the sea of ponies below and sprinkling them with rock-shaped confetti. "Welcome, everypony!" she yelled into her megaphone. "Welcome to PONYPALOOZA! You're all going to have the rockingest time EVER!" This was the biggest party she'd ever planned. It was so thrilling!

"Yaaay, Ponypalooza!" Fluttershy yelled quietly, flying beside Pinkie. Her voice was too soft for extreme cheering, but she tried her best. She landed inside the basket of the balloon and turned to Pinkie. "What a great turnout for the concert! You ready for your big entrance?"

They had the whole thing planned out. Pinkie would land onstage, thank the guests for coming, and tell them about the rock farm. Then the concert would begin, and everypony would rock the night away!

"You betcha-wetcha, Fluttershy!" Pinkie yelled into her megaphone. It was so loud that it caused Fluttershy's pink hair to blow backward in a gust of wind. Fluttershy winced. "Whoopsies!" Pinkie giggled, moving the megaphone away from her face. "Sorry, got a little *carried* away!"

"It's okay!" Fluttershy said, taking off again. "I'll see you down there soon, Pinkie!"

A few moments later, Fluttershy arrived at the front entrance. It was decorated with several large rock piles, bunches of rock-shaped balloons, and a festive banner. Twilight and the others were there, wearing their all-access badges. Pinkie Pie's family stood beside them, watching as the hordes of eager attendees entered the field. There was a buzz in the air, and it wasn't just the happy bees that were flitting around in the fragrant flowers.

"This is going to be sweet!" a tall royal-blue stallion yelled to his pack of buddies. "I can't believe Pinkie Pie got Coldhay to perform! They are totally my favorite band of all time!"

"Yeah, and I heard they are going to do a set with the Whooves," said his beefy red stallion friend with a guitar cutie mark. "It will go down in Equestria history as the most rad performance ever!"

Just after them, a group of giggling mares wearing matching shirts all trotted inside. "When does John Mare go on? I'm so in love with him."

Igneous Rock's eyes were wide with disbelief. "How did our little Pinkamena do all this? I've never seen so many ponies in my whole life!"

Igneous turned to his wife, who also looked shocked. Cloudy's jaw was practically on the ground. "And they all came out to help us?"

"What did I tell you?" Twilight smiled knowingly. "You have a very special daughter. She sure knows how to bring ponies together." Twilight turned to Rarity and whispered under her breath, "Now, let's just hope it works!"

"Oh, it will, darling," said Rarity, winking. She was full of giddiness and excitement herself. For a social butterfly like Rarity, this was heaven. "It will!"

The two ponies hoof-bumped and ran off to their assigned stations. It was almost time to get this rock party started!

CHAPTER 15

The Rockin' Ponypalooza Party!

✦ ✦ ✦

Just inside the front entrance, Applejack was working the cider and apple rock cake booth. "Come get 'em! Apple rock cakes! Pie family secret recipe!" she hollered to the crowds. She really didn't need to try very hard to sell them. Cloudy Quartz had helped her with the recipe, and the cakes were delicious. So far, the concertgoers were buying them faster than Applejack could dish them out! They'd already sold two whole batches, and the show hadn't even started yet. "Giddyup, Apple Bloom! Bring out another batch!"

"Got it, sis!" the little filly replied with an excited smile, and ran off to do as she was told. Sweetie Belle and Scootaloo followed her. "We'll help, too!"

Near the stage, Rainbow Dash was pumping up the crowd with some awesome Wonderbolt-style tricks. She dived into a barrel roll and flew right above the hundreds of ponies. Then she landed on the stage and hoof-bumped a white pony with a blue streaked mane and sunglasses. It was none other than DJ Pon-3, who was busy spinning some beats to get the party started on her turntable.

Suddenly, a couple of Coldhay's road-ponies burst through the crowd and ran toward the stage.

"Go for Casper!" a white stallion in a headset shouted, and was quickly followed by a young Pegasus doing the same. "Go for Razzi! T minus three minutes to showtime! Let's go, everypony!" Whispers of excitement rippled through the crowd, and everypony stamped their hooves on the ground.

The sun was just starting to set over Ponyville as Pinkie Pie's balloon floated down onto the stage. DJ Pon-3 transitioned to a new song as Pinkie hopped out of the basket.

"Fillies and gentlecolts of Equestria!" Pinkie Pie shouted into her megaphone. "I'm Pinkie Pie, and I'm here to welcome you to . . . the first annual Pinkie Pie Family Rock Farm Ponypalooza Party!" The ponies went wild with cheers. Pinkie bounced and flipped all over the stage. "Let me ask you this: Do you love rocks?! I know I do!" Pinkie screamed into the megaphone. The crowd started chanting *rock* over and over. "Wahooooooo! Are you ready to rock?!"

"Yeah!" the crowd yelled back.

"All right, let's goooooo! Please welcome Canterlot's very own . . . COLDHAY!!!!" Pinkie Pie welcomed the band and waved to the crowd as she exited.

By the end of the night, it was Pinkie's name that the ponies were all chanting. It was the most fun she'd ever had—because she was being herself and nopony else. It rocked.

CHAPTER 16

A Rockin' Success

★ ★ ★

Over the next few days, all anypony could talk about was the rockin' success of the Pinkie Pie Family Rock Farm Ponypalooza concert. The performances had been stellar; the ponies had danced all night. And most important of all, they were reminded of how totally awesome rocks were!

It was incredible how the rock farm had gone from struggling to thriving overnight. Igneous and Cloudy were taking orders for front path stones, cottage bricks, and even pet rocks! It seemed like everypony wanted something! Cloudy and Igneous couldn't *stop* smiling.

When it was time for them to go home, Pinkie Pie and her friends gathered to wish them a safe journey. "How can we ever thank you, Pinkie?" Igneous Rock said to his daughter. Cloudy and Pinkie's sisters stood nearby with wide smiles on their faces. "You saved the farm!"

"I could never have done it without the help of my friends... and you guys!" Pinkie giggled. "Wasn't it a fantilly-astically great time?!"

"Abso-tootley-lutely!" answered her dad

with a wink. "Be sure to come and visit us on the farm, now! Your mother's birthday is coming up real soon."

"A birthday?!" Pinkie's eyes grew wide and she did a little kick. "You know what that calls for?"

"A party!!" everypony chorused.

"Hey! How'd you guys know what I was gonna say?!" said Pinkie Pie.

We dare you to read

my LITTLE PONY Rainbow Dash

Exclusive GIANT trading card inside!

and the

Daring Do Double Dare

by G. M. Berrow

Coming Soon!

Wait! There's more . . .

Turn the page for a
special surprise from
Pinkie Pie!

Dear reader,

I put together these rockin'
bonus pages just for you!
Have a ponyriffic time filling
them out and sharing them
with your friends!

your friend,
Pinkie Pie

PARTY-PLANNING WORD SEARCH

Pinkie Pie needs help finding some items to get ready for the Spring-Sproing-Spring Party. Can you help her by circling the words below?

U	G	A	G	E	T	S	N	B	S
E	N	I	L	O	P	M	A	R	T
S	I	U	O	Y	C	L	E	L	B
D	R	T	F	G	L	M	T	N	B
N	P	M	T	O	A	N	D	M	P
E	S	A	O	E	E	G	N	U	B
I	N	N	R	R	F	E	G	F	A
R	S	T	U	T	R	N	C	L	D
F	S	R	U	A	Y	T	O	T	S
E	Q	S	A	N	C	S	T	C	C

BALLOONS BUNGEE CONFETTI
FRIENDS FUN PARTY SPRING
STREAMERS TRAMPOLINE

BIRTHDAY MIX-UP

Pinkie Pie is planning a birthday party for Rarity, but she accidentally dropped the bag. Now her invitations are all mixed up! Help her sort out the guest list by unscrambling the names below.

1. WETEISE LLEBE

_ _ _ _ _ _ _   _ _ _ _ _

2. AINRBWO SHAD

_ _ _ _ _ _ _   _ _ _ _

3. LEIEREECH

_ _ _ _ _ _ _ _ _

4. JCAPAPKLE

_ _ _ _ _ _ _ _ _

5. UTTREFLYHS

_ _ _ _ _ _ _ _ _ _

6. LTIGHWIT PRASKEL

_ _ _ _ _ _ _ _   _ _ _ _ _ _ _

7. NOB BNO

_ _ _   _ _ _

Rockin' Field Study

Pinkie Pie grew up on the family rock farm. It was tough, but while she was there, she also learned about different types of rocks and how much fun they can be! She even turned some of them into pets! Have an adult help you collect some rocks from the park or your own garden. Use the space below to record your findings. Rocks totally rock!

Draw It!

Rock Name: _____

_____

Color: _____

Location Found: _____

_____

. . . .

Draw It!

Rock Name: _____

_____

Color: _____

Location Found: _____

_____

Draw It!

Rock Name: _____

_____

Color: _____

Location Found: _____

_____

....

Draw It!

Rock Name: _____

_____

Color: _____

Location Found: _____

_____

....

Draw It!

Rock Name: _____

_____

Color: _____

Location Found: _____

_____

AWESOME COSTUMES

*The ponies of Ponyville love to play dress-up—
especially for costume parties. Have you ever
worn a costume? What did it look like?
What made it so special?*

_____

_____

_____

_____

_____

_____

_____

_____

Rock On Playlist

No party is complete without music!
Use the space below to list your favorite
party songs for a rockin' playlist.

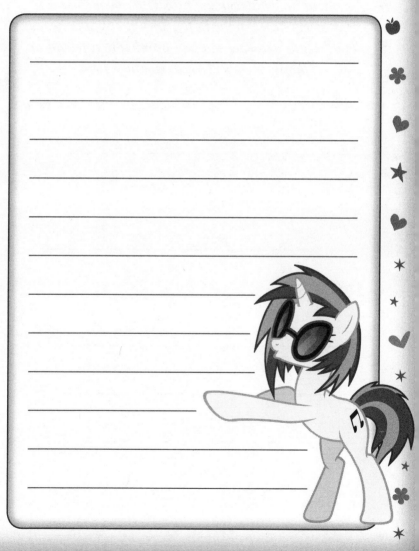

PINKIE PROMISES

Whenever Pinkie Pie feels super-duper strongly about something, she makes a Pinkie Promise. That means she will do whatever she promised when she said, "Cross my heart, hope to fly, stick a cupcake in my eye!" Have you ever made a promise to a friend or family member? Write about it here.

DRAW THE TAIL ON THE PONY

*One of Pinkie Pie's favoritest party games
of all time is Pin the Tail on the Pony!
Help these ponies find their tails again by drawing
them. Be sure to make them pretty, silly, kooky—
or whatever you can dream up!*

PARTY CANNON PREDICAMENT

Pinkie Pie's party cannon is going crazy! Decorations from the wrong holidays are all over Ponyville! Help the ponies set things straight by matching the decorations below with the correct holiday.

Hearth's Warming Eve

Hearts and Hooves Day

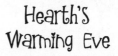

Gummy's Birthday

Nightmare Night

Too Many Pinkie Pies!

Pinkie Pie wanted to make sure she didn't miss out on any fun in Ponyville, so she cloned herself in the Mirror Pool. Now there are too many Pinkie Pies! Circle the true Pinkie Pie below.

LIMESTONE AND MARBLE PIE'S CONNECT THE ROCKS

Pinkie's sisters, Limestone and Marble Pie, work on the family rock farm. They love to spend their days mining for rocks and just hanging out together. Sometimes, they push the rocks into a pattern to make a picture. Connect the rocks below to find out what they've made!

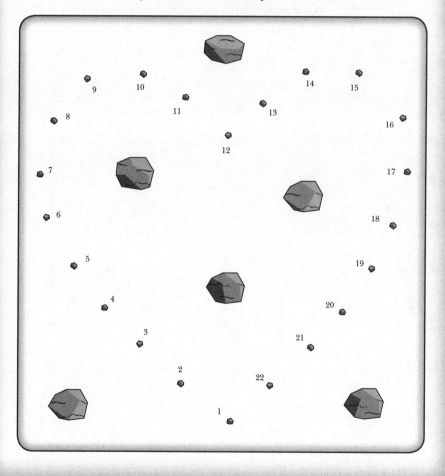

PLAN A PINKIE-PERFECT PARTY!

If you were going to plan a party just like Pinkie Pie's, how would you do it? Would you decorate with purple balloons or green flags? Would you serve cupcakes or carrot sticks? Use the space below to plan your very own party!

Party Name: _____

_____

Occasion: _____

_____

Guest List: _____

_____

_____

_____

_____